Also by David McKee:
Elmer and Rose
Elmer and Super El
Elmer and the Big Bird
Elmer and the Birthday Quake
Elmer and the Hippos
Elmer and the Rainbow
Elmer's Christmas
Elmer's First Counting Book
Elmer's Opposites
Elmer's Special Day

American edition published in 2013 by Andersen Press USA,
an imprint of Andersen Press Ltd.
www.andersenpressusa.com

First published in Great Britain in 2004 by Andersen Press Ltd.,
20 Vauxhall Bridge Road, London SW1V 2SA.
Published in Australia by Random House Australia Pty.,
Level 3, 100 Pacific Highway, North Sydney, NSW 2060.

Distributed in the United States and Canada by
Lerner Publishing Group, Inc.
241 First Avenue North
Minneapolis, MN 55401 U.S.A.
www.lernerbooks.com

Color separated in Switzerland by Photolitho AG, Zürich.
Printed and bound in Malaysia by Tien Wah Press.
David McKee has used gouache in this book.

Library of Congress Cataloging-in-Publication Data Available.
ISBN: 978–1–4677–2033–5
ISBN: 978–1–4677–2040–3 (eBook)

1 – TWP – 3/27/13

This book has been printed on acid-free paper

ELMER
and SNAKE

David McKee

Andersen Press USA

Elmer, the patchwork elephant, was thinking.
He was thinking that it was a nice day for doing nothing.
Nearby were two other elephants. "Look," whispered one.
"Elmer is thinking up a trick to play on us. Let's play a
trick on him instead."
"What shall we do?" asked the other elephant.
"I don't know. I can never think of tricks,"
said the first. "But Snake will know."
Off they went to see Snake.

"Hello, Snake," they said. "We want to play a trick on Elmer. What can we do?"

Snake thought, then chuckled. "Tell him he's looking pale. Get him to lie down and rest."

"He'll see that *that's* not true," said one of the elephants. Snake sniggered. "If it's repeated often enough he'll believe it. You'll see."

The elephants weren't convinced – but they agreed to try Snake's idea because they didn't have any other. On the way home they asked other animals to help them fool Elmer.

Meanwhile, Snake snuck off and told Elmer the idea. "Do as they say, Elmer, and lie down where you usually do," he said. "I'll bring some white mud from the pool and rub you with it. It will make you look pale. They want to trick you, but we'll trick them."

"All right, Snake," said Elmer. "I feel like lying down and doing nothing. I'll have a walk first."

Soon after, Elmer met Leopard who said,
"Are you feeling all right, Elmer? You look pale."
"Do I?" said Elmer. "Oh dear!"
Then every animal that Elmer met said,
"Are you feeling all right, Elmer? You look pale."
And Elmer said, "Do I? Oh dear!"

While Elmer returned to the other elephants,
Snake was busy dragging a very large leaf
towards Elmer's favourite lying-down place.
On the leaf was a pile of white mud.

"Here comes Elmer," the elephants whispered to each other. Then out loud they said, "Are you feeling all right, Elmer? You look pale. You should lie down and rest." Elmer just nodded and went to his usual place.
"It's working," chuckled the elephants.

Snake was ready and, using a smaller leaf, covered Elmer with a thin coat of mud. Elmer giggled.

"Stop, they'll notice," said Snake, then finished and hid. Elmer was left with his colors looking paler under the thin coat of mud.

"I'll go and peek at Elmer," said an elephant.
Elmer was asleep. Being covered with mud
is relaxing, especially when you feel like
doing nothing.
The elephant returned to the others.
"He's very quiet," he said. "And
he really does look pale."

The elephants laughed. One said, "Snake said that if we told Elmer often enough he'd believe it. Now you're believing it, too. Go and look again."

While they were talking, Snake gently covered Elmer with more mud. Elmer slept on.

The elephant found Elmer paler than ever and hurried away to get the others. Snake covered Elmer yet again then hid as the elephants arrived.

"He's getting paler all the time," said the first elephant. "What shall we do?"

"We'll have to ask Snake," said another.

Snake heard and hurried home.

When the elephants arrived, Snake was waiting.
He acted surprised, "Believing you are ill can make you
ill," he said. "The way to cure Elmer is to tickle him."
At first the elephants were shocked, but Snake convinced
them, and they hurried away to try the cure.

Elmer awoke feeling strange. The mud had
dried, making a stiff cover all over him.
At the same time, the elephants tiptoed up and started
to tickle him. Elmer laughed and jumped up, bursting
out of his mud shell like a chick breaking out of an
egg. His colors showed as brightly as ever.
"Hurrah!" shouted the elephants. "It worked.
Snake was right."

Elmer laughed. "Snake? He's a crafty one!
You thought you were tricking me, I thought I was tricking
you, and Snake tricked all of us. It's Snake we should tickle."
But Snake, being sensible, had gone on vacation.
So the elephants tickled each other and anyone else that was
around, until the jungle rocked with the sound of laughter.

4/27/18 - 7/9/18
11/2/18 - 11/5/18